FUN CAMPFIRE STORIES

John Bradshaw

John Bradshaw's website; www.eaglewingsbradshaw.com
Other published works: FUN CAMPFIRE GHOST STORIES,
FUN CAMPFIRE STORES ANTHOLOGY

Printed in the United States of America

First Printing: 2009 Eagle Wings Publishing

ISBN- 978-0-557-17897-1

Eagle Wings Publications

Dedicated to

Adam, Christopher, Spencer
and Alicia

Thank you Rookie for not eating the draft.

FUN CAMPFIRE STORIES

Contents

Before we get started

Campfire style stories have been enjoyed by generations of listeners. It is an American tradition. FUN CAMPFIRE STORIES is a collection of short campfire style tales that have a fun ending. Some are original and others are variations of stories that have been told around campfires for years. This book continues the tradition of FUN CAMPFIRE GHOST STORIES. All the stories are imagination filled, some have suspenseful story lines that combine with humor and end in a non-threatening way. All of them are fun.

Everybody loves good short stories around the campfire. There's something mystical about the unknown, something fun about imagining encounters with the supernatural. The words fire the imagination. Try to tailor the story to a setting or location that the audience can relate to. The presentation is more important than the content. Pre-reading the story is a must for the story teller. Recital through memorization is the best. Acting out the story with expressions and jesters along with voice tone changes, make for a memorable event.

The listener's mind draws pictures of the people and events in the story. The story does not have to be very detailed to be successful. The listener does not have to know what color shirt the character is wearing or the color of his hair. The story teller paints word pictures in the mind of the listener. If the teller can make the listener "see" what is happening, then the story is a success.

This collection continues the spirit of stories that relieve the suspenseful build up of the storyline with a fun ending. Kids might even say that the story was silly or not scary, but ask if they would like another and the response is invariably a hearty "Yes."

Always remember your audience. Some stories maybe too intense for some younger listeners.

My goal is an entertaining and fun campfire story telling event.

So enough of this other stuff. Let's get to the meat and potatoes. Is it dark? Is the fire going? Are you ready? Are you really ready?

Ok, here we go.

Are you ready for a story?

Eyes

Summertime is the best time. Logan was having a fantastic time at camp. This had been the first summer that Logan went to camp with a few of his buddies from school. They were all in the same cabin and had just spent their first day shooting a gun at the rifle range, shooting an arrow with a bow at the archery range, riding horses and swimming in the lake. They looked forward to the next two weeks of exciting activities.

The camp was beautiful. Set in the foothills of the Great Smoky Mountains, Camp Carlisle had everything. There were numerous cabins that housed about ten campers each and a counselor. The cabins were scattered amongst the pine trees around a central green yard that stretched down to the private fifteen acre lake. Behind the cabins were numerous activity areas, such as a gym where they played dodge ball, an arts and crafts center where they were going to make lanyards and clay pots and a campfire ring for night activities and campfire stories.

The camp was actually built from an old deserted mining town dating back to the 1860s. The thought of that is cool, Logan said to himself. The first question that comes to mind is; why was the town deserted? Logan's counselor, Randy, said that he would explain it later. When we went horseback riding, the stable guy told us that the stables used to be a train station and the path through the woods that they rode on was the old train track bed.

Anyway, Logan and his friends were back in their cabin getting ready for the dinner bell. They had just returned from the washhouse where they got their showers and were looking forward to a filling meal in the camp cafeteria. Logan's friends were hoping that their evening would include a few ghost stories. Logan said that he had heard some stories were really scary. His friends started to make fun of him saying, *"Logan is afraid of ghost stories."*

"I am not!" Logan responded. *"You mean to tell me that you guys have never heard a story that made you shiver?"*

"No, ghost stories are not real, they are made up," Michael said.

Timmy chimed in, *"We're not afraid of ghost stories. They are all silly. They are fun to hear, but we are not afraid of them."*

Then Michael and Timmy started chanting, *"Logan is afraid...Logan is afraid...Logan is afraid."*

Their taunting was interrupted by the sound of the dinner bell.

After dinner, there was the evening swim just as the sun moved behind the hills. After the swim, the campers proceeded to the council ring where a huge fire roared. There they sang songs, played some games and had a great time. The only thing missing was a ghost story. On the way back to the cabin, Logan's friends made their counselor promise to tell a story after lights-out. They looked at Logan and said, *"We hope it doesn't scare Logan that much."* Logan just shook his head.

Back in the cabin, Logan and his buddies changed into their pjs and climbed under their sheets.

Taps started to play over the loud speaker signaling that it was lights-out time. Randy turned out the cabin lights and said, *"Are you guys really ready for a ghost story...a true ghost story?"*

Michael snickered, *"Yea...right...a true ghost story."*

Randy said that everyone had to be quiet if he was going to tell the story. Silence fell upon the cabin as Randy continued.

"You guys know that this camp was built where there was once an old deserted town, but do you know why it was deserted long ago? Well, there used to be a train that came through town, you guys know the station was where the stables are now. Anyway, the train did not always stop in town, but it would always drop off and pick up the mail. When the train came through town, a man on the train would throw a bag of mail off and grab a bag of mail that was suspended on a hook at the station as it sped by.

One day, the man on the train threw off the mail bag and, just as he was reaching out to grab the mail bag off the hook, a couple of kids went running behind him and bumped the man out a little further. The hook that the mail bag was on caught the man at the side of his head and ripped his eyes out.

The man never forgave the kids for making him blind. The story goes that the man was a hermit in the woods for many years and slowly developed a type of sonar. He would repeat the words - EYES...EYES and anybody who had their eyes open, he could find. At night he would come into town and snatch the eyeballs out of people's heads and try to fit them back into his own eye sockets. In the morning they would find the poor victims, many in their own beds, with their eyes torn out and the eyeballs smashed up in the corner where he threw them after trying to put them in his own head.

The town's people were powerless to stop the slaughter that happened every night, so they deserted the town. Many years later, when the camp was just being built, there were some workmen staying in one of the cabins. Late one dark night, they heard, EYES...EYES...I NEED EYES. All of the workmen were killed, their eyes removed and smashed up in the corner of the cabin, except for one guy, who had become so sacred that he had shut his eyes hard and kept them closed the whole time.

This gave the police a theory that might end up in the capture of this deranged animal. Their plan was to put a couple of policeman in the cabin at night. If EYES came they would shut their eyes tightly. Their theory was that when their eyes were shut the creature's sonar would not work and he would stumble around as a blind man. Then the rest of the police force would charge in from the cabin up the hill and capture the killer.

Late that moonless night, the policemen heard in the distance a voice, - EYES...EYES...I NEED EYES...They remained silent as the sound got closer, EYES...EYES...I NEED EYES... Within moments the sound was in the cabin, - EYES...EYES...I NEED EYES. The policeman closed their eyes and kept them closed as the monster started to stumble around the cabin. The rest of the police force rushed down the hill from their hiding place and ordered the dark figure to stop, but the creature ran out the back door towards the woods. The policemen drew their weapons and fired.

The next morning all they found was some globs of green blood heading off into the thick woods."

"Is that a true story?" Michael asked.

"So they say," was Randy's response.

Randy said that he had to go to the counselor's lodge for a few minutes and instructed the campers to stay quite and go to sleep.

Wow, that was a good story, Logan thought. Just as Randy left the cabin, Logan remembered that he had not brushed his teeth so he quietly got up and went to the washhouse. The lights over the water basins had a lot of bugs flying around them. Just as Logan finished brushing his teeth, he felt a stinging pain on his right arm. He looked down just in time to see a bee fly away. It had left it's stinger in Logan's arm. Logan pulled it out and, remembering his first aid class, knew that if he got some ice on it quickly it would not hurt as much.

As he got closer to his cabin he called out, ICE...ICE...I NEED ICE. As he opened the door to the cabin he yelled out again, - ICE...ICE...I NEED ICE. As Logan turned on the cabin light, he heard screams like little girls would make and his buddies, Michael and Timmy, shivering under their sheets with their eyes tightly clenched shut.

"Look who never gets scared!" Logan said, pointing at Michael and Timmy.

Stars

Joe and Bill loved camping. It was their chance to get away from all the pressures of normal living. Out in the woods, they could relax and enjoy nature, instead of dwell in the constant headaches of the man made world they were forced to spend most of their time in. Out in the woods, it was all natural.

They hiked until they found an isolated spot deep in the forest. They set up their tent, rolled out their sleeping bags, gathered wood and started a fire.

After a filling dinner, they propped themselves on an old log and enjoyed the heat and light of the campfire as shadows danced off the canopy of trees.

Joe took out his book, FUN CAMPFIRE GHOST STORIES, and Joe and Bill took turns reading some of the stories out loud. This was the life! It was a peaceful, calm and beautiful night away from people, crime and problems.

The night wore on and the fire slowly burned down to a glowing mound of embers, when they crawled in their tent and fell sound asleep.

Some hours later, Joe woke up and stared at the night sky for several minutes. Joe reached over and shook his friend awake and said, *"Bill, look up at the sky and tell me what you see."*

Bill replied, *"I see millions of stars."*

"What does that tell you?" asked Joe.

Bill pondered the question for a minute and then he said, *"Astronomically speaking, it tells me that there are millions of galaxies, and potentially billions of planets.*

Astrologically, it tells me that Saturn is in Leo. Time wise, it appears to be approximately a quarter past three in the morning.

Theologically, it's evident the Lord is all-powerful and we are small and insignificant.

Meteorologically, it seems we will have a beautiful day tomorrow.

What does it tell you, Joe?"

Joe was silent for a moment, then said, *"Bill, you stupid moron, someone has stolen our tent."*

The skeleton

The Gault Middle School had been closed for over ten years. Tomorrow it was scheduled for demolition, but today was clean-out day.

John, Alicia, Cindy and Dennis were high school students. They were hired for a weekend job along with others to make one final inspection of the old deserted middle school for any possible items of value to be salvaged before the wrecking ball arrived.

The rumor was that one of its students disappeared from the school just over ten years before, never to be heard of again. In spite of a city wide search, Ben was never located. Some said that he never left the school, but was now part of the building, haunting it forever...or until it was reduced to rubble. Others said that the school was closed because of his disappearance or because it was haunted, but the official reports said that it was closed due to budget concerns.

John, Alicia, Cindy and Dennis spent most of Saturday morning going from one room to the next. They looked in all the corners and in all the closets. There was little of any value found. Some old books, a broken desk or two, and some dilapidated chalkboards, were the greatest finds. One thing that really caught their interest was a scraping on a wall next to a closet door. It said, *"Ben was here."*

How creepy, they thought. *"What if the story was true?"* John said. Dennis said, *"There are no such things as ghosts."* Alicia said, *"Don't you remember those strange sightings of a strange glow at night coming from rooms in the building?"* *"Yea, probably just vandals or vagrants roaming the halls or seeking shelter,"* Cindy said as they moved to a new room.

Dennis opened the door on a small cupboard in the corner of the next room and said, *"Wow, that's really weird...look."* Scratched in the wood on the inside of the cabinet were the words, *"Ben was here."*

Within the next few hours, the group found numerous places, hard to get too places, that had the same inscription, *"Ben was here."* It gave everybody there a strange creepy feeling. Their minds were preoccupied with the thought of Ben and where he might be.

Dennis said, *"What do you think happened to Ben?"*

"I think he was kidnapped by a stranger who took him far away," Cindy responded.

John chimed in, *"I think he was killed and buried in the walls of the school by bullies. I think he wanders the halls at night for his vengeance. I think they closed the school out of fear that the ghost of Ben would do harm to other students...I'm just kidding, BOOO!"*

A nervous laughter came from the group as the setting sun became evident by the rising shadow on the walls. *"One more room left,"* Alicia said. *"Let's get it done and get out of here."*

The last room on the hall was an old broom closet. They opened the door and looked inside.

There was nothing of note, but an old rusty bucket and a broken mop. *"Let's get out of here,"* Dennis said.

"Wait a minute," Cindy said. *"Look at that rug in the back. That might be worth something."*

Alicia pulled the dusty rug out and the group turned to leave when John noticed something on the floor. It looked like the floorboard was cut, but on a closer examination, it appeared to be a door in the floor. It was a trap door of some sort.

"Look at that," John said.

"Open it," Dennis said.

John picked up the broken mop handle and shoved the end under the edge of the trap door. He was able to pull it up enough to get his fingers under it. He threw the lid open quickly, because he did not like the idea if his fingers, unprotected, under that lid.

The lid hit the back of the storage room wall with a thud. Dust blew in all directions. After a minute the dust settled.

An unsettled feeling feel over the group as they saw the words, *"Ben is here,"* scratched into the inside lid of the trap door.

Cindy broke the silence, *"Well who is going to look inside?"*

Dennis said, *"It's your turn Cindy!"*

Cindy slowly stepped toward the opening in the floor. She peered in, but it was still dark. After a few moments, she could see and what see saw caused her to scream and back away from the opening quickly. Her response surprised the others and they became apprehensive.

"It's a skeleton!" Cindy screamed.

Everyone stood motionless for what seemed like an hour. John moved toward the opening and looked in. *"Yep, it's a skeleton alright."*

Alicia and Dennis looked inside the dark hole to see for themselves.

Noticing the clothing, Alicia saw that there was some sort of medal or pin attached to the cloths that hung on the bleached white bones.

John took the medal off the tattered shirt and read the inscription, *"Ben, 1999 Hide and Seek Champion."*

A letter from camp

S ometimes, the scary stuff is for the parents at home.

Dear Mom,

Our scout master told us all to write to our parents in case you saw the flood on TV and worried. We are OK. Only one of our tents and two sleeping bags got washed away. Luckily, none of us got drowned because we were all up on the mountain looking for Chad when it happened. Oh yes, please call Chad's mother and tell her he is OK. He can't write because of the cast. I got to ride in one of the search & rescue jeeps. It was neat. We never would have found him in the dark if it hadn't been for the lightning. Scoutmaster Webb got mad at Chad for going on a hike alone without telling anyone. Chad said he did tell him, but it was during the fire so he probably didn't hear him.

Did you know that if you put gas on a fire, the gas can will blow up? The wet wood still didn't burn, but one of our tents did along with some of our clothes. John is going to look weird until his hair grows back. We will be home on Saturday if Scoutmaster Webb gets the car fixed. It wasn't his fault about the wreck. The brakes worked OK when we left. Scoutmaster Webb said that a car that old you have to expect something to break down; that's probably why he can't get insurance on it. We think it's a neat car. He doesn't care if we get it dirty, and if it's hot, sometimes he lets us ride on the tailgate. It gets pretty hot with ten people in a car. He let us take turns riding in the trailer until the highway patrolman stopped and talked to us.

Scoutmaster Webb is a neat guy. Don't worry, he is a good driver. In fact, he is teaching Terry how to drive. But he only lets him drive on the mountain roads where there isn't any traffic. All we ever see up there are logging trucks. This morning all of the guys were diving off the rocks and swimming out in the lake. Scoutmaster Webb wouldn't let me because I can't swim and Chad was afraid he would sink because of his cast, so he let us take the canoe across the lake. It was great. You can still see some of the trees under the water from the flood. Scoutmaster Webb isn't crabby like some scoutmasters. He didn't even get mad about the life jackets. He has to spend a lot of time working on the car so we are trying not to cause him any trouble.

Guess what? We've all passed our first aid merit badges. When Dave dove in the lake and cut his arm, we got to see how a tourniquet works. Also Wade and I threw up. Scoutmaster Webb said it probably was just food poisoning from the leftover chicken. He said they got sick that way with the food they ate in prison. I'm so glad he got out and became our scoutmaster. He said he figured out how to get things done better while doing his time.

I have to go now. We are going into town to mail our letters and attend the gun and knife show.

Don't worry about anything. We are fine.

Love,
Cole

P.S. How long has it been since I had a tetanus shot?

Boom! Boom! Boom!

"*What on earth was that?*" Spencer said, as he lay in his bed, not daring to breathe.

Boom! Boom! Boom!

There it was again. It sounded like a loud, dull knocking on the front door.

Boom! Boom! Boom!

It was the end of October and Spencer was just ten years old. His parents had gone to dinner and a movie. *"You are so big now,"* They said. *"You don't need a babysitter anymore."*

I'm all alone, Spencer thought. What if somebody tried to break-in? I'm defenseless.

Boom! Boom! Boom!

For a moment, Spencer felt a sense of relief as he thought that maybe, it was his parents who were knocking at the door. He looked at the clock. It was only 8:34 and was actually far too early because his Mom said that the movie would not be over until 10:00. And, obviously, his parents had a front door key.

But what if they have lost the key? What if they are standing in front of the door and could not get in. Spencer's stomach started to feel quezzy.

"What should I do now?"

He felt totally helpless. Dad had made him promise not to open the door when he was home alone. You could never know who wanted to get in. Maybe it was a drunken tramp or a robber. Or even worse, maybe it was an evil vampire who was creeping through the darkness to fulfill his hunger with fresh blood, he thought as his heart almost skipped a beat.

He kept as quiet as possible so that the monster at the door would not hear him. He listened to the darkness as if he was under a spell.

Spencer's mind turned to the comfortable feeling that his parents might be standing at the locked front door. He could not stay in bed any longer.

Vampire or not, I don't have any other choice but to get up and see who keeps knocking at the door, Spencer concluded. Worrying about his Mom and Dad was worse than the fear of an uninvited visitor.

Spencer crept along on his tiptoes and crawled along the floor to the window which is right next to the door. He slowly pushed the curtain to one side and cautiously looked out through the window. Nothing and no one was there, just the pitch black darkness of the night.

"Phew!" His knees stopped shaking with fear. No reason for panic. There is no one outside and no one wants to do me any harm. He thought as he calmed himself down.

"No vampire, no intruder, but no parents either," He said quietly. *"I would feel better if Mom*

and Dad were home now." Spencer went into the kitchen and got a glass of milk. Milk always helped him sleep better.

Everything is OK. The movie will be over at 10:00 and they will be home in a couple of hours. Whoever knocked on the door was not there anymore. It was probably our neighbor, Mr. Miller or another of his parent's friends, Spencer thought as he headed back to the warmth and security of his bed.

He went back upstairs and climbed into bed. Everything was peacefully as he slowly fell asleep. Spencer slept like a bear until suddenly,

Boom! Boom! Boom!

Oh no! Whoever or whatever wants to get into the house has come back again. Fear engulfed him, sweat formed on his brow and the little hairs on the back of his neck tingled. Spencer hid under the covers shaking. Maybe it was just a dream, he thought. Moments later,

Boom! Boom! Boom!

Spencer worked up the courage to crawl to the bedroom window. He knew he had to be quiet. As he slowly peeked through the window blinds, he was horrified to see two figures in black at the front door.

Boom! Boom! Boom!

Spencer could just stare at the dark figures as they turned and disappeared into the darkness.

Spencer ran to the phone and called his Mom's cell phone, but he just got her voice mail. He realized that she had to turn it off in the movies. What should he do?

Boom! Boom! Boom!

Spencer went back to the window and peeked out. Now there were four or five creepy creatures at the door.

Boom! Boom! Boom!

Spencer ran to the phone and called his neighbor, Mr. Wilson. *"Please answer, please answer the phone,"* Spencer said as the phone rang. *"Hello, this is Mr. Wilson."*

"Mr. Wilson, this is Spencer from next door. I'm at home by myself and there is somebody pounding on my door tiring to get in. I'm scared."

"I'll be right over Spencer. Just hang on for a second."

Boom! Boom! Boom!

"Mr. Wilson, please hurry!"

Spencer went back to the window. He had never felt fear like this before and he did not like it. Suddenly, he saw Mr. Wilson coming up the front path. Spencer ran downstairs as fast as he could to the front door. He unlocked it and as it opened, he almost screamed. Standing in front of him were three menacing monsters. Standing behind the monsters was Mr. Wilson.

"Spencer," he said. *"It's OK, everything is alright. You must have forgotten that it is Halloween."*

Poor Rufus II

In Blackwater Swamp there was know to exist a colony of strange, lizard like creatures that fed on other animals in the swamp. Occasionally, they would come out of the swamp at night and devour farm animals and unsuspecting pets in the surrounding countryside. These creatures stood like a human, but were much more powerful. They had alligator type teeth and only ate raw red meat.

Over many years, these demon creatures had slowly been killed, one by one, by the farmers that bordered the swamp and by hunters, unsuccessfully tiring to display the creatures for all to see. The creatures were never captured alive and, when they were killed, they dissolved into swamp gunk almost immediately.

Doctors surmised that the creatures might have the cure to swamp fever in their blood and they desperately wanted to capture one of the creatures so they could make a serum that would cure or prevent swamp fever in animals and people.

The creatures had been hunted down until just one was left. If they could capture the last one, than there might be hope for a cure. No one was foolish enough to venture into the swamp and this last creature never left the swamp. They decided that they needed to find a witless man that would take the chance to capture the monster.

They ran an ad in the paper that said they would pay five hundred dollars to anyone that could capture alive the last creature of Blackwater Swamp. Only one person responded to the ad.

Remember Rufus from FUN CAMPFIRE GHOST STORIES? Well, Rufus had just been released from the hospital after blowing off his toes in that haunted house. He had lost out on five hundred dollars so he decided to get it back by doing this job.

If you don't remember, Rufus lived in a dirt floor shack on the outskirts of town. He never had a real job and never wanted one. He was the town derelict. He had dropped out of school in the sixth grade, had lost most of his teeth, his cloths were always dirty and he was always on the lookout for an easy dollar. He had taken a job that would pay five hundred dollars if he stayed in a haunted house overnight. Rufus, blew is toes off with his own shotgun and was not able to complete the job.

Anyway, the doctor's group hired Rufus for the job. Rufus would get five hundred dollars if he captured the creature alive. Once he captured the creature, he was to call the doctor's group on a cell phone that they gave him. The doctor's group would then come and pickup the creature.

Nothing could be easier. Rufus thought. *"No one is going to cheat me out of my five hundred dollars."*

Rufus borrowed a bear trap and some beef jerky from a guy on the other side of town by the name of Mark, who had three sons. Rufus headed off into the swamp with his trap, cell phone, beef jerky and his shotgun.

"No one is going to cheat me out of my five hundred dollars," Rufus said as he set out the trap and put the beef jerky in and around it.

Rufus hid behind an old log for hours swatting mosquitoes and squashing large beetles. All he could think about was the five hundred dollars. Boy…he could live a couple of years off that kind of money.

Early the next morning, Rufus was nodding off to sleep when all of a sudden, SNAP! CLAMP! Rufus jumped up and, to his delight, saw the lizard monster trapped in his trap face down in the swamp. Rufus gleefully started to celebrate. *"Five hundred dollars…five hundred dollars…I'm getting five hundred dollars!"*

Rufus ran over to the creature with a big toothless smile on his face. He stared at the motionless body and his smile slowly turned into a frown. Rufus poked at the creature with his shotgun, but it did not move. He yelled at it, *"Hey, you critter, move. You better not be dead! No one is going to cheat me out of my five hundred dollars!"*

After several minutes of yelling and poking, the creature still did not move. Rufus began to fear that it might be dead so he decided to use the cell phone and get directions from the command center where the doctors eagerly awaited news of a live capture.

Rufus walked a few feet away until he got a good signal and then punched the preprogrammed number and the phone rang. One of the doctors answered. Rufus said that he had captured the creature in a trap, but it was not moving and he thought it might be dead. *"But can I still get my five hundred dollars?"* Rufus said.

The doctor knew that if the creature was dead it would have dissolved into swamp gunk. He asked Rufus if he could see the creature. Rufus said that he had to walk away to get a good signal on the phone and was not able to see the creature from where he was standing.

The doctor said, *"Well first thing we have to do is make sure it's dead."*

"Will do," Rufus said without hesitating as he put the phone down on a log.

"Rufus...Rufus," the doctor called out on the phone. *"Rufus, if it's there, it is alive. RUFUS..."* But Rufus was no longer on the phone.

In the distance, the doctor on the phone heard Rufus say, *"Looks like I'm going to get my five hundred dollars after all."* Then there was a large shotgun blast...BANG!

A few moments later, Rufus got back on the phone and said, *"Ok now what?"*

The old house

This story is designed for story telling

The old house had made noises before, but this was different.

Adam had lived there for many years. The house was old when he bought it and he knew it like a glove. He knew when the temperature change between day and night would cause the old brick to expand and contract causing snaps and groans in the old house. He knew where each creaky floorboard was and he knew which door would moan when it opened or closed. Tonight however, was different. There was something else going on.

Adam returned from work and made himself dinner. After dinner he retired to his comfortable lounge chair next to the fire. The expected rain began to fall outside in the darkness, which made the crackling of the warm fire all that more comfortable. Adam kicked off his shoes and took his favorite book from the nightstand and began to read. It was not long before the sound of the rain on the old house's tin roof and the warm fire brought sleep over him.

THUMP!

Suddenly, Adam was awakened in a startled state by the noise. *"What was that?"* He listened for the sound again, but heard nothing except the rain on the roof. The fire had burned down to a lightly glowing mound of embers. His eyes wandering around the room as he soon discovered the source of the sound. The book he was reading had fallen on the floor from his lap. The comfortable feeling of an explanation caused Adam to relax back into the molded comfort of his recliner.

BANG! THUMP!

Adam's eyes sprung open. The rain was harder now and the flashes of lightning would momentarily light up the room. Another flash and Adam started to count...one thousand one, one thousand two, one thousand three, one thousand and four, BOOM! He knew that counting the time between the flash and the boom could give him an estimate of how far away or how close the lightning was. A count of four meant the lightning was about a mile away. Another flash and...one thousand one, one thousand two, one BOOM! The lightning was now only about a half mile away. It was getting closer.

CREEEK!

Adam knew that sound. It was that floorboard upstairs in the hall that he had walked over so many times. What could have caused it to creek? No one else was in the house or no one else was supposed to be inside the house! That sound only happened if the floorboard had been stepped on. Adam slowly got up from his chair and grabbed the fireplace poker. Since he was in his stocking feet, he made no noise as he slowly climbed the stairs. When he got to the top of the stairs, Adam reached out for the light switch and turned it on. He turned it off and back on. The light would not come on. The storm must have knocked out the electricity. His flashlight was downstairs in the kitchen. Adam slowly backed down the stairs.

In the kitchen, Adam fumbled through the catch-all drawer for the flashlight.

There it was, he thought as he switched it on. Disappointment overwhelmed him has a barely visible yellowish light glowed from the business end and got progressively duller. Dadgumit, the batteries needed to be replaced. Why had he not done that?

FLASH! BANG! THUMP!

The kitchen filled with light for a split second. The deafening sound of the thunder was right with it. The sound was so sharp that Adam instinctively ducked. The storm was right on top of the house now. That thump came from the bedroom above the kitchen. Adam reached for the phone, but it was dead. He grabbed a candle from the catch-all drawer and took a knife from the counter. Adam stuck the wick of the candle into the embers of the fire and lightly blew until the wick ignited. With the candle and knife, Adam headed upstairs again.

The rain was falling hard now and the sound of it hitting the old house's tin roof was loud. The wind picked up and that old shutter that Adam had planned to fix started to bang against the side of the house. Lightning flashed with the quick response of thunder as Adam made his way slowly down the hall.

CREEEK!

Adam stepped on the loose board. He paused for a moment and then continued toward the bedroom above the kitchen.

FLASH! FLASH! BOOOOM!

The thunder, lightning and wind were at their peak now. He could see the tree out of the window ahead, thrashing against the window pane. The flashes of lightning gave it a menacing look as it moved and cast weird shadows on the hallway wall. Adam's comfortable house was now strangely different. He felt insecure, he felt afraid.

Without warning, there was a large howl of wind and a large wet tree limb broke through the upstairs hall window just ahead of Adam. The rain was blowing in from the broken window as the wet tree limp still moved in the wind as if it was alive.

THUMP! THUMP!

The sound was coming from just beyond the tree. Whatever it was, it was just behind the broken limb. The rain blowing in the window soaked Adam as he slowly moved closer. The cold water, dripping down his face and chest gave him a chill. The wind was causing movement all around. The candle blew out. Adam clutched tight the knife in his hand. He moved closer to the branch in order to peer beyond it.

Adam reached out to part the swaying leaves when, suddenly, he SCREAMED LOUDLY! (At this point, scream loudly and then do and say nothing. Someone will eventually say, *"What happened? "*)

Your response will be: *You would scream too if you stepped on some broken glass in your stocking feet!*

BC

Mrs. Linderfelt was a lady who was rather old-fashioned, always quite delicate and elegant, especially in her language. She and her husband were planning a week long vacation in Florida, so she wrote to a particular campground asking for a reservation. She wanted to make sure the campground was fully equipped, but didn't quite know how to ask about the toilet facilities. She just couldn't bring herself to write the word "toilet" in her letter. After much deliberation, she finally came up with the old-fashioned term BATHROOM

COMMODE. But when she wrote that down she still thought she was being too forward. So she started all over again, rewrote the entire letter referring to the bathroom commode merely as the BC. She wrote, *"Does the campground have its own BC?"*

Well, the campground owner, Rick Smith wasn't old-fashioned at all and when he got the letter, he just couldn't figure out what the woman was talking about. That BC business really stumped him. After worrying about it for awhile, he showed the letter to several campers, but they couldn't imagine what the lady meant either. So Rick finally came to the conclusion that the lady must be asking about the local Baptist Church, so he sat down and wrote the following reply:

Dear Madam:
I regret very much the delay in answering your letter, but I now take pleasure in informing you that a BC is located nine miles north of the campground and is capable of seating 250 people at one time. I admit it is quite a distance away, if you are in the habit of going regularly, but no doubt you will be pleased to know that a great number of people take their lunches along and make a day of it. They usually arrive early and stay late. It is such a beautiful facility and the acoustics are marvelous...even the smallest sounds can be heard quite well by all. The last time my wife and I went was six years ago, and it was so crowded we had to

stand up the whole time we were there. It may interest you to know that right now a supper is planned to raise money to buy more seats. They are going to hold it in the basement of the BC. I would like to say it pains me very much not to be able to go more regularly, but it surely is no lack of desire on my part. As we grow old, it seems to be more of an effort, particularly in cold weather. If you do decide to come down to our campground, perhaps I could go with you the first time, sit with you and introduce you to all the other folks. Remember, this is a friendly community.

Sincerely, Rick Smith

Deathbed

Peter was a well known music composer. Later in life, he had written seven musical ballads that had been well received by the community. He stopped composing when he fell sick. Peter had been very sick for a long time. The Doctor had long since said that he had done all that could be done. Peter was not long for this world, but it seemed that people where waiting for and almost wanting his demise.

"No...that could not be, you say?"

Well, how about the other day when the doorbell rang and Marcie, his wife, answered the door. Peter was sick, but he could still hear what was going on. Mr. Humphries was at the door. He was the local undertaker and gravedigger. Marcie asked Mr. Humphries how he was doing and he said, *"Very poorly, very poorly. I haven't buried a living soul in the past six weeks. Oh, by the way, how is Peter doing?"* Marcie responded that Peter was expected to go any hour now.

Later that day, Peter smelled the unmistakable aroma of fresh baked chocolate chip cookies. Peter was near death, but chocolate chip cookies were his favorite. He summoned the energy to climb out of bed and slowly made his way to the kitchen where his faithful wife was baking his most favorite treat. He spotted some cookies fresh out of the oven on the counter. He moved toward the counter and put out his hand to pick up a warm, delicious cookie. Suddenly, Marcie slapped his hand with the spatula and said, *"Don't touch them. They are for the funeral."*

Depressed, he made his way back to bed and died.

A popular man, Peter left Marcie strict instructions in his will for his wake to be a jolly and happy affair: a celebration of his life. To this end, Peter had left $52,000 dollars in his will for the party.

As the guests left at the end of the wake, Marcie was asked by her close friend, Alicia, if she thought that Peter would have been pleased. *"Well, I'm sure Peter would have been delighted,"* Marcie murmured.

"I'm sure you're right," replied her friend, Alicia, who lowered her voice and leaned in close. *"How much did all this really cost?"*

"All of it," Marcie said, *"Every penny of the $52,000 dollars."*

"What!" exclaimed Alicia in a higher than normal voice, *"I mean, it was very nice, but $52,000 dollars?"*

Marcia took a deep breath and answered, *"Look, Alicia, let me explain: the funeral cost $15,500. I donated $1,500 to the church. The wake, food and drinks were another $5,500. The rest went on the memorial stone."*

Alicia worked out the math in her head, *"Eh?"* she exploded for a second time, *"$29,500 for a memorial stone? My goodness, how big is it?"*

Marcie shows Alicia her ring finger, *"Oh about 30 carats,"* she smiled.

Later that week, there were reports of music coming from the graveyard. After an hour they were able to narrow down where it was coming from. It appeared that the music was coming from Peter's grave. Marcie and her friends, along with a slew of curious bystanders, stood next to Peter's gravesite and listened to the music. Marcie soon recognized the music as Peter's ballads except they were being played in reverse. This was a complete mystery until the undertaker, Mr. Humphries, arrived. He explained that Peter was just decomposing.

The flower lady

Happy Hills Nursing Home was a nice three story retirement complex that housed several hundred people. The top floor was usually reserved for the residents that required the most care. The entire complex was modern, bright and cheery.

Mary Wells was a resident of Happy Hills who also volunteered her time working on the third floor. She would help the nurses with the residents and she would spend time with the more sickly. She was best known as the flower lady because she spent most of her time delivering fresh cut flowers to every room on the third floor. She always said that flowers made her feel better and she loved sharing that feeling with her friends on the top floor.

When Mary was not delivering flowers, she was busy in her little flower garden on the back part of the complex. Mary spent so much time working with and handling flowers that she always smelled like flowers. Folks on the third floor could smell her coming down the hall before she arrived and the sweet smell of flowers stayed in the air long after she left. Everyone was grateful that Mary was there.

One night in January, Mary could not sleep so she decided to go up to the third floor and see if any of the residents were up and wanted company. When she arrived, she noticed some smoke slipping out from under the furnace room door. She opened the door and was immediately confronted with a room on fire. The opening of the door allowed oxygen to rush into the room and fuel the fire. It was too hot to close the door. Mary almost panicked, but then she remembered the residents on the floor. Mary notified the night nurse on duty and pulled the fire alarm. She rushed from room to room helping the residents to the elevator before returning to a new room and doing the same. As she worked to clear the floor, the fire grew and the ceiling was filling with thick dark smoke. She finally got the last resident to the elevator where she and the nurse joined the resident as the elevator doors slowly closed. Just as the doors were about to shut, Mary pushed the open button and told the nurse to go down and she would be right there. The nurse pleaded with Mary to get back on the elevator, but Mary said she had to get something real quick.

The doors to the elevator closed and Mary ran back down the darkening, smoke filled hallway. She got to the nurses station and grabbed the beautiful flower arrangement she had left there earlier that day. She was heading back to the elevator, but the smoke was so heavy that she was having trouble seeing and breathing. By the time she got back to the elevator she was coughing and feeling faint. She pushed the button on the elevator, but because of the fire it had stopped working.

The firemen finally put the fire out saving the rest of the complex, but the third floor had been destroyed and the only fatality was Mary Wells.

Over the next several months the third floor was renovated and was due to open in just a couple of weeks. One night, the night watchman Tim was making his rounds on the deserted third floor when he smelled the aroma of flowers. The smell instantly reminded him of Mary and this gave him pause. He continued his rounds as he thought that his mind was playing tricks on him. Later that night, Tim's partner

Ted returned to the guardhouse after making his rounds, including the third floor. Upon his return he reported to Tim that all was well. Then Ted mentioned the smell of flowers up on the third floor. Tim looked up at him and said, *"What did you say?"*

Ted again said, *"Yea, I was making my rounds on the third floor and it smelled like a flower garden. When I walked by room number seven, I even heard a sound like sisssss. At first I thought that someone was there, but I was all alone."*

A few nights later, Tim headed up to the deserted third floor. The work had been completed and the new Grand Opening of the third floor was only a couple of days away. As the elevator doors opened, the only light on the floor was a few emergency lights. Tim quietly headed down the hallway. Suddenly, Tim stopped in his tracks. Tim got a faint whiff of flowers.

Could it be Mary? He would love to see Mary again, but he was not interested in seeing a ghost. Every ghost he had heard about was scary. Should he tell management? Would they believe him? It sure is dark in here, he thought. Tim pulled his flashlight out from his utility belt and turned it on. He shinned the light down the hall, but saw nothing unusual.

Tim checked out rooms one, two and three. All was normal except the smell of flowers seemed to get stronger. Rooms four and five checked out fine, but just as Tim stepped back into the hallway, he could hear the faint *sissss* sound that Ted said he heard a few nights before. Tim had not heard that sound before. The smell of flowers was even stronger now. Tim shinned his light down the hall toward room six.

Tim slowly moved toward the room in a crouched position. Arriving at the door, he quickly turned the corner and shinned his light from one side of the room to the other.

Everything was normal, but there was the bathroom door which was closed. Tim moved to the bathroom door, slowly placed his hand on the handle, turned it and quickly opened the door. Tim had a feeling of relief as he found nothing unusual. As he headed back to the door to the room, he heard it again, *sissss*. Tim knew the sound came from room seven.

The smell of flowers filled the air. Tim wanted to leave, but he knew that his job required him to find out what was going on. Tim walked along the hallway wall toward room seven. He stopped every couple of feet to listen. Silence was all he heard, but the smell of flowers was the strongest there. Tim turned the corner from the hall into room seven. His flashlight beam moved from side to side of the room searching. Tim's heart was pounding in his chest.

There is something there. He heard it. He could smell it. What was it?

Suddenly, right above his head, Tim heard *sissss*. Tim almost wet his pants. Whatever it was, it was right over him. Tim slowly raised his eyes and slowly followed with the beam steaming from his flashlight.

There it was. Tim could not believe it. The ghost of Mary...was an automatic air freshener mounted on the wall above the door.

The bronze ghost

B en was a lonely guy. He stayed to himself and had few friends. As much as he would like to have a girlfriend, he could never work up the courage to ask a lady out on a date. Ben lived in a low rent single room apartment. He made little money as a street cleaner, but he did love ghost stories.

One night, Ben was looking for something to do, so he left his dingy room and walked down the street. It was a nice night so Ben kept walking and walking. After a while, Ben realized that he was walking in a part of town he had never seen before. A cold breeze went down his shirt collar and he looked up at the clouds gathering overhead. He figured that it was time to turn back. Just then, he saw a light that caught his eye. It was a flickering neon light over a storefront in a building where all the other storefronts were boarded up and dark. Ben knew that it was way too late for a store to be open, but he was curious what the store was.

As he moved closer, he could see the light flickering the name, "Wo Fong's Curios and Artifacts." As Ben approached the storefront, he became amazed at the sight of hundreds of different items jammed in the dusty store windows. He pressed his face against the dirty glass and noticed a little old man behind the counter. No, it could not be … but as he turned the door knob, the door opened. Ben walked in and the old man said, *"Welcome to Wo Fong's. Make yourself at home, please browse around and take your time. I am sure you will find something that will interest you."*

Ben spent an hour looking. Most of the things in the store looked as if they had been there a very long time. Look at that! Ben thought as he moved toward a shelving unit at the back of the store. On the bottom shelf was the most fascinating thing he had ever seen. It was a beautiful bronze statue of a ghost. I have to have this, he thought, but do I have enough money? Ben carried the statue up to the counter where the old man was sitting on an old stool.

"How much is this sculpture?" Ben asked.

"Aw...you have found a very special item. Only one like it in the whole world. The sculpture is only ten dollars, but the story behind it will cost you a thousand dollars."

"Forget the story, but here is the ten dollars." Ben said as he handed over the money. He could not believe his luck. He would have paid twice as much for it.

As Ben exited the store, the store lights went off and he could hear the door lock. The wind had picked up and it had become noticeably cooler. It was very dark and the city was silent. Ben started his long walk back to his dingy apartment when, all of a sudden, a strange noise came from the dark alley on the other side of the road. Ben paused for a moment when, out of the darkness, came a shadowy figure making a moaning sound and moving toward Ben. Ben quickened his pace as the ghostly essence followed.

As Ben passed the next side street, a skeleton with ragged clothing, crawled out of the sewer and joined the chase after Ben. Ben started to jog as he heard the moaning and the clacking of bone against the pavement in pursuit. Ben looked over his shoulder and was startled to see that several more ghostly creatures had joined the chase. A ghoulish monster climbed out of a foul smelling dumpster and made a heart stopping growl as it too seemed focused on Ben.

Soon there were at least a dozen ghosts, goblins and other foul creatures following Ben. Ben did not know what to do. He was so frightened that he had lost his way and did not know where he was. All he knew was, as he ran on and on, more horrific beings were coming out of their dark hiding places and chasing after him. He also knew that, sooner or later, he would not be able to run anymore and the mob of supernatural demons would be upon him. If he could just find some help, but there was no one there. Ben was alone, his fate too terrible to think about.

Ben soon found himself running on a road leading out of town. The creatures were slowly getting closer as Ben's energy waned. In the darkness, through the trees, Ben spotted a glowing fire. Maybe someone was there. Maybe it was a campsite. Ben ran as fast as he could toward the fire. Unseen tree branches slapped his face and tore his cloths as he got closer to the fire.

Finally, he emerged from the trees and entered the campsite. The foul monsters were now only a few feet away. What should I do now? he thought. Then Ben had a revelation. He threw the bronze ghost statue into the campfire and ducked behind the tree on his left.

The ghosts, monsters, ghouls and goblins all followed the statue into the fire and were consumed, turning into dark smoke that rose to the tree tops and then dissipated by the breeze.

Ben was exhausted, bruised and battered, but he knew what he must do. It was near dawn when Ben arrived back at the storefront of "Wo Fong's Curios and Artifacts." Unbelievably, the neon light was on and the store was open. Ben stumbled into the store and was greeted by the old man behind the counter.

"I see that you have come back. Perhaps you want the story behind the statue you purchased last night?" The old man said confidently.

"No...forget that." Ben said.

"I want to know if you have any special statues of beautiful women."

I'm not who you think I am

In high school, I needed money. I was able to drive, had a girlfriend, and liked to go out with my friends. My folks didn't have much money and I needed to pay my own way. I had worked at restaurants and grocery stores and wanted to try something more interesting. While searching around, I stopped at the zoo.

As it turned out, the zoo director liked my style and said he had an interesting job that he felt I could handle. We walked through the back alleys and tunnels of the zoo that most people never see until we got to the gorilla cage, but it was empty.

The director told me that their gorilla, named Kong, had caught a bug and was in quarantine for the next week. Kong was getting old and they were, even now, shopping around for a replacement. Kong just sits on a tree branch holding onto a rope all day. When the crowds started arriving on the weekend, they'd be disappointed to have no gorilla since everyone enjoys the gorilla exhibit, even a boring old gorilla.

The director said he had a gorilla suit I could wear if I would be interested in sitting on the branch for four hours at a time so the people would have something to look at. It sounded good to me, not the usual high school job, so I told him I would.

The next day I went to the zoo, put on the gorilla suit and climbed into the cage. I sat on the branch holding the rope and soon there was a crowd of children pressing their faces to the bars.

It didn't take long for me to start getting bored, so I started to scratch my armpits, thump my chest, and twirled the rope. About an hour passed and I began to really get into this gorilla thing. I would grab the rope and swing across the cage. The kids thought it was great so I started swinging higher and higher.

In the next cage there was a lion and he was becoming irritated by my antics. He began to pace in his cage and roar. I kept swinging and started to swing to the lion's side of the cage. I would use my feet to push off of his bars. As I swung out farther, he would roar even louder. It was, actually, a lot of fun and the kids were really enjoying the show.

All of a sudden, I missed the bars, flew through them and dropped right into the lion's cage! I landed on my back and was stunned, but immediately got up and ran to the front of the cage where the crowd was.

"Help me, help me, I'm not who you think I am!" I screamed.

Just as I yelled, the lion jumped on my back and knocked me to the ground. His head was at my neck and I was sure I'd never make it to graduation.

Then he whispered in my ear, *"Shut up stupid, or you'll get us both fired."*

Our first night in a tent

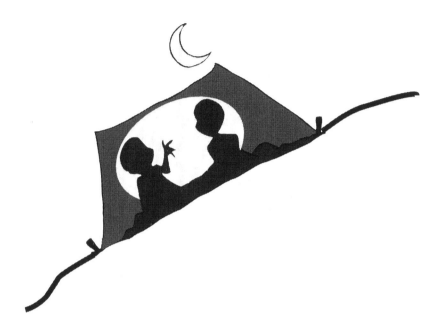

In a place where a mountain goat might lose its footing, we put our tent up high on a slope. A gust of wind could have blown it from the side of the hill, but we were happy that it stood at all, so we climbed inside. A wet cold seeped out of the ground. It was our first night in a tent. We were 12 years old and we thought everything was as it should be.

As it got darker, the cold gave us goose bumps. The crescent moon peeped out between the forested mountains and, in the fading light, I saw a man walking towards our tent. He was still a long way away. His outline was blurred by the mist that covered the ground.

I became so frightened by the appearance, that for a moment I was unable to move. The wind played a game with the mist and the grass, which swayed in the moonlight and changed shape.

The man soon seemed to change into a giant bear which stood and stared at our tent. Then it seemed to change into a little evil gremlin which silently crept towards us.

I finally managed to utter the name of my friend. *"Jason, I see something!"* Jason thought that I had had a nightmare. *"Where?"* He said as he rolled over and looked outside.

"I don't see anything," he said, obviously relieved.

His calmness seemed to be catching. Maybe the whole thing was just a bad dream?

I looked out again and there the creature stood, threateningly. I tensed up again.

"He's coming! Can't you see him, Jason?" I whispered. Jason peeked out attentively in the same

direction. A bolt of fear shook through his body and I knew that he had seen the evil gremlin too. *"He's coming towards us!"* Jason said in a low voice.

"Be quiet! Maybe he will walk by us if he doesn't hear us!" We stared so long that our eyes started to water. It seemed like hours that the thing stood in the same spot. Then it gradually moved two or three steps closer.

The moon faded. The first sleepy bird twitter came out of the valley and the sky hung over the slope with a mild light. The gremlin slowly bent over and a large drop of water fell from its nose. I stared wildly at the creature for several more stained minutes as the light brightened the hill slope.

As detail became more defined in the light, we discovered that our creature was actually a tall clump of grass about ten feet from our tent. Jason and I crawled out of the tent and stomped on the clump of grass that kept us awake all night. We had survived our first night in a tent!

Things aren't always as they seem.

Once upon a time, there was a very poor farmer that was down on his luck. He had sold off most of his livestock to pay his property taxes and soon had to resort to selling parts of his property.

One day, the tax collector came to the farmer and told him that if he gave him the two acres to the south that bordered the new high end subdivision, he would delay collecting the farmer's taxes for one year. The tax collector said that he was going to build an expensive house on the old foundation that was there. The farmer did not want to give away the property, especially since it was the location of the old family house that had burned down during the civil war, but he had little choice.

The tax collector was a selfish, greedy man. He knew that the farmer would not be able to pay is taxes now or in the future and he would be able to get all the property for a steal. The farmer agreed, but with one stipulation; that if the tax collector abandoned the property before the next tax bill was payable, it would revert back to him.

Within six months the ruthless tax collector had built a beautiful new mansion on the foundation of the farmer's old homestead.

Two traveling angels stopped to spend the night in the home of the tax collector. The tax collector's family was rude and refused to let the angels stay in the mansion's guest room. Instead, the angels were given a small space in the cold basement. As they made their bed on the hard floor, the older angel saw a hole in the wall and repaired it. When the younger angel asked why, the older angel replied, *"Things aren't always as they seem."*

The next night the pair came to rest at the house of the very poor, but very hospitable farmer and his wife. After sharing what little food they had, the couple let the angels sleep in their bed where they could have a good night's rest.

When the sun came up the next morning, the angels found the farmer and his wife in tears. Their only cow, whose milk had been their sole income, lay dead in the field.

The younger angel was infuriated and asked the older angel, *"How could you have let this happen? The first man had everything, yet you helped him. The second family had little, but was willing to share everything and you let their cow die."*

"Things aren't always as they seem," the older angel replied. *"When we stayed in the basement of the mansion, I noticed there was gold stored in that hole in the wall. Since the owner was so obsessed with greed and unwilling to share his good fortune, I sealed the wall so he wouldn't find it."*

"Then last night, as we slept in the farmer's bed during that terrible thunderstorm, the angel of death came for his wife. I gave him the cow instead. Lightning struck the tax collector's house and it burnt down to the foundation. The heat cracked the foundation wall exposing the gold within, which now belongs to the farmer and his wife. Things aren't always as they seem."

Let's go fishing.

Planning a fishing trip in the wilds takes a lot of planning. Charlie and Leonard were amateurs when it came to camping and fishing, but there's a first time for everything. They spent months planning their two night adventure. They found a perfect spot along the bank of beautiful Carson Creek.

They went to the outfitter's store and spent four thousand dollars buying sleeping bags, a tent, backpacks, cooking gear, fly rods, tackle, fishing vests and waders. They spent three hundred dollars each on out of state fishing licenses. They filled up the truck with gas, another fifty bucks, and spent two hundred more dollars on food, drink, flashlights and sun block.

Soon the day of departure arrived. It was a beautiful day as Charlie and Leonard packed the truck and headed down the road toward Carson Creek wilderness. About one hundred miles down the road the truck had a flat tire. Unfortunately, Leonard had taken the spare out to make room for all the gear. Charlie had to call a tow truck that cost one hundred dollars to tow the truck to the nearest shop. After getting a new tire mounted and buying a spare, the pair were set back another three hundred dollars.

It was late afternoon when Charlie and Leonard pulled the truck into the trailhead parking lot. They loaded up with their gear and started down the trail. Since they were behind schedule, it got dark quickly and the buddies found it harder to follow the trail at night. It started to rain and continued to rain on and off until morning when Charlie and Leonard, exhausted and wet, finally arrived at their campsite.

They spent the morning drying out their gear, setting up their tent and looking at the beautiful creek. Although they were tired, they looked forward to getting out in the creek right after they gathered some firewood and had lunch.

Charlie and Leonard went into the surrounding woods to gather firewood. Charlie got a big splinter in is right hand from an old log and Leonard received a bite from a spider he did not see under another log.

They were both famished since they had not eaten a bite since the day before so they planned on a big, hot lunch. Unfortunately, the wood was wet and so were the matches so the pair had to make do on a couple of cans of SPAM.

After lunch they put their waders and fishing vests on, grabbed their rods and stepped into the creek. Ok, things had not gone quite as planned up to this point, but it would be all good from this point forward, they thought.

The babbling creek was beautiful. The water was crystal clear as it flowed over smooth rocks. Thank goodness they had spent the extra money on insulated waders since the water was so cold. It took some time for Charlie and Leonard to get their casting skills refined enough to have a chance at success. Leonard was becoming self-assured as he told Charlie to, *"Watch this cast!"* Leonard drew back his rod and flicked his fly back, which lodged its hook into Charlie's waders. Upon executing a powerful forward thrust with his rod, the hook tore a seven inch long opening in the waders which promptly filled with near ice cold water.

Charlie fished from the bank the rest of the afternoon without success due to the fly constantly catching the trees. Leonard had equal luck on his continued attempts. It was late afternoon when the friends returned to their campsite. They soon discovered that an animal of some sort had discovered their food. There was little left except some crushed cans of SPAM.

Leonard started a fire, while Charlie decided to take one last cast from the bank before dark. There was a tug on the rod and the fight was on. Leonard cheered Charlie on as he reeled the monster in. After a hard fought battle, Charlie landed a rainbow trout that had to be close to four inches long. *"At least we have some real meat for dinner."* Charlie said.

Charlie and Leonard finished their dinner of SPAM and four bites each of fresh trout. Leonard didn't even mind the fishbone that pierced his cheek. Darkness engulfed the campsite except for the flickering flames of the fire as the stars shined brighter than the friends had ever seen. *"This is what it's all about,"* they said. Tomorrow they would take turns using the waders and rake them in.

Charlie and Leonard crawled into the tent and zipped up their sleeping bags for a good night's sleep. The owl in the tree over the tent was really loud, but heck it's the sound of nature. Speaking of nature, Leonard had the call of nature and had to relieve himself. Not thinking, he only went a foot or two outside the tent and peed on the small hill above the tent. The liquid ran down hill and saturated a nearby fire ant mound. The ants became aggravated and soon found the tent to attack. Their swarms soon found the entrance and with in a couple of minutes, Charlie and Leonard were yelling and jumping around the campsite in their underwear, swatting ants of their body parts. No going back to the tent that night, so the friends wrapped up in their ponchos and lay down on the hard ground next to the now nonexistent fire.

Even though they were exhausted, sleep was a commodity hard to come by that night. Their backs hurt from the hard ground, it was cold and the owl's hoots were not conducive to sleep.

As the sun rose the next morning, the sore, exhausted and hungry friends became determined to catch fish. Charlie's hand was throbbing from the splinter and the spider bite had caused a nasty bump on Leonard, but rainbow trout was on the menu. Since they had fished up creek the day before, they decided to go downstream. Charlie used the waders first while Leonard watched from the bank. At midday they switched. By the end of the day they were done. Not a single bite!

As they returned to their camp, they saw that the animal visitor from the day before had returned and took the rest of their food. All of the SPAM, that they thought to secure inside the tent, was gone and the tattered remnants of the tent stood as a testament to the short battle. The friends laid their rods by the bank as they surveyed the scene.

No food, no fish, no tent, thank God they were out of there in the morning. Leonard looked for the matches, but they were nowhere to be found. Clouds gathered and the rain began to fall. Charlie and Leonard huddled under their ponchos under the tall pine on the small hill overlooking the campsite. It got dark, it got cold and the rain got harder. Soon the friends watched as the swelling creek became a river and washed away their rods, backpacks and the rest of their gear.

Late the next morning, Charlie and Leonard made it back to the trailhead parking lot. What a welcome site, until the friends got close enough to the truck to discover the broken window and the missing radio and spare tire.

The trip home was quite except when the silence was broken by Charlie who said, *"Can you believe that we spent over five thousand dollars for one lousy undersized fish?"*

After a short pause, Leonard said, *"Thank goodness we only caught one!"*

The special one

Sara had studied hard and worked hard, but finally her day was here. She had always wanted to be a Doctor, not just any Doctor, but an animal Doctor. She was graduating Veterinary school and had been offered a job by the county. She graduated with honors and the next day showed up at the county offices.

Sara was briefed on her new responsibilities by the retiring Veterinarian, Dr. Russell. She learned that her responsibilities included making the rounds at the farms in the county once a week to assist the farmers as best she could.

Her first week on the job was mostly uneventful; the usual horse vaccinations, sprained dog paws, and sick cows. However, when she got to the Dudley farm, she saw something extraordinary.

While she was talking to farmer Dudley, a pig came ambling around the corner of the barn. What was extraordinary about it was that the pig had three artificial legs!

Sara asked farmer Dudley about this curious sight. Why would anybody give a pig even one artificial leg, much less three?

"Well," he drawled, *"that there ain't no ordinary pig. Let me tell you. One day I was out baling some hay, and I hopped off the tractor to check the tire, which was kind a wobbly. Wouldn't cha know it, the tractor started to roll of its own accord, and trapped me right there under the wheel. Just then old Pinky the pig wandered by and saw what happened. She skedaddled back to the house and fastened her teeth on my wife's apron and wouldn't let go until he dragged her out to where I was layin'. Luckily, my wife was able to get the tractor off me."*

Sara was quite impressed. She knew that pigs were pretty intelligent, but she had never heard of a pig doing anything like that. *"That's amazing,"* she said, *"But that still doesn't explain the artificial limbs."*

Dudley said. *"My son was down at the swimin' hole over yonder a couple summers ago. He hit his head on a big log out in the middle of the pond. He was about to go down for the third time, when old Pinky jumped into the water, swam out to him, grabbed him by the shorts with her teeth, and drug him coughing and spluttering up onto the bank. Saved my son's life, that pig did."*

"Incredible!" she exclaimed. *"Most pigs can't even swim! But the artificial legs...?"*

"Well, last year the old farmhouse burned down," Dudley continued. *"We were all asleep when the fire started, but old Pinky ran squealing around the house 'til we all woke up. She even went and dragged my youngest daughter from her bedroom just seconds before the roof collapsed."*

"That's one special pig," Sara said, *"but please, tell me, why does Pinky have three artificial legs?"*

"Well," said farmer Dudley, *"a pig like that's just too good to eat all at once."*

Parkside Road ghost

Parkside Road had a reputation. It was an old county dirt road that was once an old wagon trail through the county. It was always known as a spooky road, because it was a lonely road that few people traveled and it bordered a swamp that generated a heavy fog that would blanket the road at night and early in the morning.

About a month earlier, a rumor started to go around town that a ghost had been spotted on the road. The story was, that a ghost like figure was spotted leaning against the trunk of the huge old oak tree along side the road. The old oak was a well known landmark along the road. It was thought to be several hundred years old and had branches that stretched in all directions. This figure was spotted about nine in the evening by the minister and his wife as they walked along the road after their car broke down coming from church. They reported that the fog was rolling in from the low area so they could not get a good look at this ghostly apparition. They said that the figure did not respond to them when the minister called out a greeting, but just leered at them from the darkness under the giant oak tree. The minister's wife reported that the figure had on a cowboy type hat and appeared to have a broken noose of rope around its neck.

The minister and his wife said that the figure made a menacing movement toward them, so they turned and moved quickly in the opposite direction. When they looked back over their shoulders at the tree, the figure had vanished into the fog.

Some of the town's people thought that it might have been the ghost of a criminal that had been hung from that very tree a hundred years before.

After a couple of weeks, the story subsided until it was brought to life again, when a local farmer was using the road early one morning to take his produce to town. He reported that it was still dark and the fog was heavy, but as his wagon approached the huge oak tree, he saw the ghost with a cowboy hat on rushing out from the bushes at the end of the swamp and disappearing into the darkness under the tree. His horses became spooked and started running down the road. The farmer said that by the time he got them under control again, he had lost half this load.

People speculated that this ghastly ghost was back to take some sort of revenge on lonely travelers along this lonely stretch of road.

Michael lived in a farm house on the south end of Parkside Road. Michael's best friend Jacob lived on the north end of Parkside Road. Michael and Jacob both attended the same middle school and were very familiar with Parkside Road. Their parents had recently told the boys that they were not to travel the road by themselves since all this ghost stuff was going on.

Michael and Jacob talked about the ghost of Parkside Road while they were at school. Michael said that he was not afraid of the ghost. He said that he was mad at the ghost because it prevented him from traveling down the road to Jacob's house. Jacob, on the other hand, seemed to enjoy spreading the story around school and even adding things to it. Jacob told his friends that the ghost was trying to catch a lonely traveler, who would then take the ghost's place in the make shift gallows of the oak tree. Jacob said that he liked the old oak tree and that he had been scouting the place recently for a spot to build a secret clubhouse.

Jacob seemed to enjoy the fear that his classmates showed. Michael was the only one who did not appear to be afraid.

On the next Saturday, Michael begged his parents to let him travel down the road to Jacob's house. He promised that he would return before it got dark. His parents relented, so Michael took off towards Jacob's house. As Michael passed the old oak tree at mid-day, there was nothing menacing about it. He thought how silly everybody was. He had traveled this road a hundred times and had never seen anything more than a few deer, squirrel and an occasional possum. Michael arrived at Jacob's house unscathed and the two boys played the afternoon away. Jacob's Mom asked Michael if he would like to stay for an early dinner and Michael agreed.

At dinner, Jacob started talking about the ghost of Parkside Road. He was hoping that Michael would show some fear, but Michael just said that he was mad this story had ever started. Jacob went over to the coat rack next to the door and put on his father's hat. He looked at Michael like he thought the ghost would and said, *"BOO."* Michael and Jacob laughed until Jacob's Mom said, *"Michael...it's starting to get dark. Let me drive you home."* Michael said that he would rather walk and that his parents said it was ok. Just as Michael was heading out the door, Jacob said he hoped the ghost did not get him and that he had a secret to tell him the next day at church.

Michael started down the road, knowing it was later than he promised his parents. He quickened his pace, hoping to save some time so that his parents would not worry too long. He knew there was a shortcut from Jacob's house on a trail that intersected the road at the old oak tree, but he knew that his parents would be mad at him if he went that way through the swamp. As Michael approached the old oak tree it was dark and the fog was getting heavier. Michael slowed his approach and thought how the old tree was more daunting at night.

A few more steps on the old dusty road and Michael stopped dead in his tracks. It could not be, he thought, but there it was. Michael rubbed his eyes and opening them again was confronted with a sight that made him shiver. There, leaning up against the old oak tree, as the outline of a person...a person with a cowboy hat. It started to move toward Michael.

Thoughts rushed through Michael's head. What was he to do? Before he could decide to run, the figure was moving quicker and almost upon him.

Michael clenched his fists and jumped on the approaching figure. He swung and hit just as fast as he could, then jumped up and ran as fast as he could the rest of the way home. Luckily, his parents were still out so they did not know that he was late. Michael went to his room and, still trying to process what had happened, fell asleep.

It was a beautiful Sunday morning. Michael could not wait to tell Jacob what had happened to him the night before. Jacob and his parents would be there in an hour since the two families always went to church together. Michael decided not to tell his parents, since he was sure he would get in trouble and he also knew that they would not let him go down the road by himself again. Michael ate a big Sunday breakfast and then dressed for church.

Jacob and his family drove into Michael's driveway. When Jacob got out of the car, Michael and his family were shocked to see Jacob's black eyes and bruised face. Michael's Dad said, *"Jacob...what happened to you?"*

Jacob's Mom said that after Michael left their house the night before, Jacob grabbed his Dad's hat and rushed out of the house to catch up to Michael to tell him something. But instead of catching Michael, he had been attacked by the ghost. Jacob had beaten the thing until it vanished. They were proud of their son and knew that the bumps and bruises would heal.

The boys looked at each other and a grin formed on their faces. Michael whispered in Jacob's ear, *"I think I know now the secret you were going to tell me."* They both snickered and Jacob said, *"Yep, that ghost sure took a whooping."*

The grizzly

Tim met Christopher when Christopher married Tim's sister. Being brother in laws, Christopher tried to get along with Tim and he was always tiring hard to find a common interest between himself and Tim. Tim, on the other hand, was braggadocios know it all.

One holiday, when the family was together Christopher mentioned that he would love to go hunting sometime. Tim said that he had hunted all sorts of game, but the most fun was bear hunting.

Tim bragged that he was so good at it that he could almost catch them with his bare hands and skin them.

On the way home from the family gathering, Christopher told his wife, who was Tim's sister, about what Tim had said. She told Christopher that Tim had never been bear hunting or any type of hunting before. She was sure that Tim had never even seen a real bear before except maybe at the zoo.

Christopher still thought that this might be an opportunity for Tim and him to bond, so Christopher rented a small one room shack in the middle of bear territory during bear season. Christopher called up Tim and invited him on the trip all expenses paid. Tim agreed to go.

When Tim and Christopher reached the isolated cabin in the middle of the woods, all Tim could do was complain, complain and complain some more. The cabin was too cramped he could have found a better place. There was no electricity, no television and no phone. He did not want to cook his own food. There was no indoor plumbing, and on and on. Christopher about had his fill, but decided to grin and bear it for the sake of peace.

The next morning, Christopher got up early, got a fire going, put on the coffee and scrambled some eggs for Tim and himself. He was looking forward to getting out in the woods for a chance to see a bear. Tim just complained about how early it was and the racket that Christopher was making.

Christopher said. *"Come on Tim, lets get out in the woods and do some bear hunting. It will be a lot of fun!"*

Tim said that he did not want to go. He could skin a bear with his bare hands he had hunted bear so many times. It was no longer a challenge, but a bore. As a matter of fact, he had decided to sleep in late get up, pack up and get out of that cheap cabin and head home later that morning.

Christopher had is fill of it. *"Suit yourself,"* he told Tim as he left the cabin with his rifle.

Christopher had barely made it one hundred yards down the trail when he spotted a bear cub walking across the path ahead of him. A slight grin formed on his face as he watched the cuddly cub walking through the underbrush apparently curious about everything, but oblivious to the presence of Christopher.

Suddenly and without warning, there came a horrendously loud and ferocious growl from the path ahead of him. Standing over seven feet tall on its hind legs, a grizzle bear was growling at Christopher. It was just a few dozen yards ahead, swiping the air with its huge front paws with razor sharp claws. The bear's jaws were crammed with teeth each looking like they were a foot long.

Christopher was frozen with fear as he gazed at the menacing creature. He had not expected anything like this. His legs were trembling, but otherwise would not move. The huge grizzle lowered its front paws to the ground making an audible thud as it thrust its massive body in a run toward Christopher. Christopher raised his rifle. Sweat was dripping down his forehead and the salt was stinging his eyes. His arms were trembling just as much as his legs. He would do anything to be anywhere else at that moment. The gun went off with a BANG! The noise shocked Christopher out of his petrified state. The bear rolled into the bushes, but within a moment, Christopher knew that he was still in big trouble. The bullet had barely grazed the giant beast on the left shoulder and it had regained its footing and charged towards Christopher, even madder than before.

Christopher pulled the trigger again, but the gun jammed. He threw the rifle at the charging ton of man killer as he turned and ran as fast as he could back towards the cabin. The bear caught the rifle in its mouth and snapped it in two like it was a toothpick.

The bear was gaining on Christopher. He was shouting at the top of his lungs for Tim to help him. As Christopher got closer to the cabin, all he could hear was the thud of bear claws right behind him and Tim yelling, *"Keep it quiet, I'm trying to get some sleep in here."*

Christopher reached the front step of the cabin and slipped, falling flat on his face. The grizzle bear was too close to stop. It tripped over Christopher and rolled through the front door of the cabin. Christopher jumped to his feet and closed the door to the cabin while he yelled out to Tim, *"You skin this one, and I'll get the next one!"*

The hole

Clyde and Cletus were brothers and the best of friends. They were simple men with simple minds who lived in a pair of singlewide trailers on the outskirts of town. They grew up in a single room farm house and were educated by their mother, who only had a sixth grade education. They had no indoor plumbing and lived off the land. When their mother past away, Clyde and Cletus sold the old homestead and moved into the singlewides near town.

They took odd jobs around town to pass the time and make a little money. Some days they would help out at the church at the end of the town square, sweeping up and empting the garbage. This church had been around for a long time. An old cemetery encircled the church on two sides.

One day, the pastor of the church, Reverend Haskell, asked Clyde if he wanted a job digging a grave. The regular gravedigger was away on family business and Reverend Haskell had a burial ceremony the next morning.

Clyde had never done this type of work before, but he was sure he could help out. Reverend Haskell told Clyde that the hole had to be eight feet deep, three feet wide and six and one half feet long. He told Clyde that there was a shovel in the storage closet.

Clyde told Cletus that he was working at the church graveyard that afternoon and evening. Cletus told Clyde that he had a job cleaning up at the morgue and would not be off until around midnight. Clyde told Cletus to stop by the cemetery, since it was on his way home, and he would walk home with him unless he finished his job earlier.

Clyde got the shovel out of the storage closet and Reverend Haskell pointed to the place to dig. Clyde started to dig, but found the ground to be hard.

He realized that this hole would take some time to dig.

Meantime, Cletus was hard at work at the morgue, cleaning up. As the evening wore on and most of the employees had left for the night, Cletus found it a little creepy working around a bunch of dead bodies.

Clyde was hard at work slowly chipping away at the hard ground as the sun set and darkness approached. Just as it got to dark to see, the full moon shined through the parting clouds making it easier for Clyde to see what he was doing. Clyde continued to work into the night until the moon was overtaken by darkening clouds, making the cemetery pitch black. Clyde realized that he needed a flashlight or lantern or something to see by. He put the shovel down and turned to climb out of the hole he had dug. Suddenly, he realized that the hole was much deeper than he thought and he was unable to grab the edge of the hole even when he jumped. Clyde now knew that he was stuck in the hole until someone came by to help him out.

Just up the street, Cletus was finishing up his work mopping the floor in the morgue. The last employee had left moments before and Cletus was alone with all those dead bodies. Only fifteen minutes left until midnight and I can go home, Cletus thought as he stared at the clock on the wall. This place gives me the creeps, he thought as he looked around the now clean stainless steel tables, tubs, sinks and gadgets around the room. The clean white sheets draped over the now motionless bodies, reminded Cletus of sleeping ghosts.

Cletus looked up at the clock again and it was midnight…time to go. He put his mop back into the sink turned the light out and was glad to pull the locked door shut behind him. He pulled the collar up on his jacket, because the wind had picked up and the night air was cool. The night was very dark and, except for the rustling of tree leaves, the town was as silent as the morgue he was leaving behind. Cletus headed down the street hoping that his brother Clyde would still be at the church so they could walk home together.

Clyde was so tired from digging that he had fallen asleep confident that his brother would be there soon to help him out of the hole.

As Cletus arrived at the church, a shiver went down his spine. It was dark, the wind was unusually chilly for that time of year and the rustling of the leaves gave an eerie feel to this otherwise happy place. Clyde rounded the side of the church and slowly walked into the cemetery. *"I hope Clyde is still here, but I don't see any lights."* Cletus said quietly. Cletus almost walked into a tree it was so dark. He continued walking further into the cemetery when he was startled as a small twig fell down his jacket collar which, for just a second, felt like a finger wrapping itself around his neck. Cletus took another step and it found no ground. Cletus lost his balance and, in an instant, fell head first into a dark pit. Clyde was awakened by the thumping sound. Cletus, shaking his head, stood up and looked up. All he could see were the sides of the hole leading up to the, almost invisible, clouds rushing by. Fear over took him, when he realized he was in the ground, in the cemetery.

Suddenly, a voice said, *"There is no way out."* Cletus, hearing this, jumped ten feet into the air with fright and landed on the edge of the hole. He ran as fast as his legs would carry him out of the cemetery and all the way home, never pausing to look back.

Clyde was shocked that his brother would leave him like that in the hole. He didn't even try to help me out, he thought to himself.

The next morning Reverend Haskell found Clyde and rescued him.

Hell's fury

The old lady had just exited the store, purse in hand, when a man rushed up behind her and snatched her purse. The strap broke as the man pulled the purse away and ran through the parking lot and into the trees behind the store. The old lady was knocked over by the event, received a concussion and suffered a broken hip.

Max ran several blocks until he felt safe enough to stop and examine his loot. He propped the purse up on a pile of old tires behind the tire store and opened it up. His take for this effort amounted to twelve dollars and some change. Not what he hoped for, but better than nothing. Max than took his windfall to the drug store. He picked up a pack of gum for fifty cents, handed the young clerk a one dollar bill. When the clerk returned the change of fifty cents, Max complained that he had given the clerk a ten dollar bill and wanted his extra nine dollars in change. After the manager responded to the scene, Max was given the change that was not rightfully his.

Max had lied, cheated, swindled and stolen just about every day of his life. Max thought he was king of the streets, but at home, it was a different matter. Max went to the local bar and drank up all the money he got from the old lady and a couple of dollars his wife had given him.

Max's wife, Bertha, was a very big woman. Max and Bertha had married about five years earlier after Max had a few days of heavy drinking. Max could not even remember where he had met Bertha, but he was definitely afraid of her. Max was not a big guy and Bertha, more than once had laid Max out with a simple left cross. Max would like nothing more than to leave Bertha, but he knew that she would never allow it.

When Max arrived home, Bertha said, *"Where have you been, you no good bum? Did you bring home my cookies, like I told you?"*

"No dear." was the timid response. *"I lost the money, honey."*

Bertha stormed toward Max with her huge fists clenched. She yelled, *"I should stomp you like the insect you are! You are the worst husband, worst provider and stupidest man on the planet. I can't stand you! Did you find a job today, you wretched excuse for a man?"*

"No honey." Max said, expecting to be pummeled at any moment.

Bertha raised her huge right hand and slapped Max on the left side of his face so hard that a red hand print was left on his cheek for a few moments. She then raised the other hand and did the same for the other side of his face. *"You will get this everyday until you find a decent job, you worm scum! Do you understand me?"*

"Yes, my love." came the sobbing response.

"Now get in the kitchen and make me dinner. After dinner you will clean the dishes and get my bath ready. Remember tonight is the night you clean my toenails and drain that boil on my leg!"

After dinner, Max took the trash out to the street. It was dark and Max lived in a bad neighborhood. A man came up to Max and demanded money. Max pulled out a knife and the man shot Max dead.

Next thing Max knew, he was standing at some red gates, guarding the entrance to a fiery red tunnel. He could not go anywhere else. There was smoke all around and it was hot. Soon a red lizard with a long tail and wings appeared at the gate and opened it. *"Follow me."* it said.

Max and the flying lizard headed down the tunnel. There was molten lava seeping from the walls of the tunnel and the smell of sulfur was almost overwhelming, but at least he was not draining Bertha's boil. Soon they arrived at a desk that was engulfed in flames. Behind the desk sat a red skinned, half man, half goat creature that had a long barbed tail and blood red eyes.

"Name please?" The creature said.

"My name is Max."

"Ah yes, your name is on my reservation list. I am THE DEVIL. Now we just have to figure out where in hell you belong. Have you lied and cheated?"

Max tried, but found he was unable to lie to this creature. He confessed that he had lied and cheated. The Devil waved his claw like hand as if to say, follow me. They walked down the tunnel that now had many doors on each side. They came to a door that had a sign on it that said, - Liars and Cheaters. The Devil opened the door and inside Max saw people packed tightly together and all they could do is lie to each other for eternity. The Devil said, *"This is where you belong unless you have stolen."* Max did not want to stay in that room and he could not lie, so he was glad when he had to say, *"Yes I have stolen."*

"Then you can not stay here. Follow me." They moved down to the door marked, Thieves and the Devil opened the door. Inside were even more people packed together tighter than sardines. They were starving because they were stealing each other's food. *"In here you steel and starve for eternity,"* the Devil said. You belong in here unless you have hurt someone on purpose.

Max was glad to say that yes he had hurt people on purpose because he could not tell the creature a lie and he definitely did not want to stay in that room.

The Devil closed the door and said, *"You do not belong in this room. Follow me."*

Down the tunnel the Devil and Max went. The heat was more intense and the smell overwhelming. The sound of people screaming almost made your ears hurt. Soon they came to a door that said, People Who Hurt Other People. The Devil opened the door and inside Max saw more people than he thought could be put into a room. They were all screaming as they spent eternity hurting each other. The Devil said, *"It looks like this is where you belong, Max...unless you have scorned your wife."*

Max was unable to lie. *"Yes, I have. I have cheated on her and lied to her and wanted to leave my wretched life with her."*

The Devil motioned for Max to follow him. They descended even farther into hell. The heat was so bad that all you could do is sweat and burn. The sulfur smell burned your throat and lungs and the screams from this portion of hell were louder and longer than any other. A moment later they exited the tunnel through a back door.

The air was clear and there was no sulfur smell and the heat was gone. Just ahead of them was a beautiful white door. *"You are no longer in hell."* the Devil said. *"You belong in that room,"* as the Devil pointed his claw at the door.

"Is that heaven?" Max asked.

The Devil laughed as he opened the door marked, Scorned Women. Inside was the interior of Max's house and in the room were thousands of

Berthas all screaming at Max, all wanting to be fed, all with festering boils, all with clenched fists. *"Hell has no fury like a woman scorned. Welcome to your eternity, Max."* The Devil sneered.

The last flight

It was the day before Halloween and Matthew was trying to get home. It had been a long week at work away from home. He did not have to travel often for work and for this, he was grateful since Matthew did not like to fly. Most of the time, when he did fly, he was with an associate, but this time was different, he was alone.

Matthew finished his job a day early and he was really hoping to get home to his wife and three kids so he could enjoy Halloween with them. He arrived at the airport hoping to catch an early flight home, but all the flights were booked and all he could do was to wait stand-by.

Unfortunately, he was unable to get a seat on any of the regularly scheduled flights. Matthew stared at the departure board as the last scheduled flight of the day departed. He finally realized that he would have to spend the night there and hope to catch an earlier flight in the morning. The terminal was empty as he glanced one last time at the board. He could not believe his eyes! He looked again, an unscheduled flight showed up on the departure board and departure time was one minute after midnight. Gate thirteen was at the very end of the concourse and midnight was just five minutes away.

Matthew grabbed his carry on bag and sprinted down the concourse. As he arrived at the deserted gate, there was a sign next to the open gate door that said, Welcome Aboard. Excited that he might get home, Matthews ran down the ramp and stepped onto the plane. The door closed behind him by itself.

The airplane was dark with just a slight amount of light coming from the emergency lights. Matthew stood there for a few moments until his eyes adjusted to the dim light.

"Welcome aboard Halloween Airlines." The voice came from a figure standing in front of him.

Matthew stared at the dark figure and could slowly make out some features that made his jaw drop. Standing in front of him was a hideous creature. It was mostly skeletal, but still had some rotting skin loosely hanging on its blood stained bones. It had stringy hair and a tattered flight attendant's outfit on. Matthew saw cobwebs on the walls and ceiling, the carpet under his feet was torn and tattered and there were, what appeared to be, roaches crawling everywhere. Matthew then realized that it was Halloween and that this must be some sort of a theme flight. Well, if it got him home in time to enjoy Halloween with his family, then that was ok with him.

The scary looking figure said, *"Sir, you can take any open seat."* Matthew wondered how they got that thing to look so lifelike. It certainly could not be a costume! He turned and started to follow the emergency isle lights into the interior of the plane. His eyes were adjusting better to the dim light and he was amazed at the things he was seeing. Most of the seats were tattered and bent, the overhead bins were broken or missing, the windows appeared to have cracks in them, the carpet was torn up and there were wires and cobwebs hanging from everywhere. What he saw sitting in the few occupied seats even amazed him more. There were all sorts of strange looking creatures. In one seat there was a werewolf, in another a reptilian type swamp monster. There were skeletons everywhere and cold wispy mists floating throughout the cabin. Boy, this cost some bucks to put together, Matthew thought.

Matthew found a seat that did not have a creature or skeleton next to it and sat down. The intercom system crackled to life followed by an announcement, *"Welcome aboard Halloween Airlines, we are pleased to have some of the best pilots in the industry... Unfortunately, none of them are on this flight...! Not that it will matter, but to operate your seatbelt, insert the metal tab into the buckle, and pull tight. It works just like every other seatbelt, and if you don't know how to operate one, you probably shouldn't be out in public unsupervised at night."* Matthew reached for his seat belt, but found none. This has got to be a joke, he thought.

"In the usual event of a sudden loss of cabin pressure, oxygen masks might descend from the ceiling. Stop screaming, grab the nearest mask too you and pull it over your face. If you have a small child traveling with you, secure your mask first before assisting with theirs. If you are traveling with two or more small children, decide now which one you love the most.

There are no operating emergency exits and since our flight will be over rock hard solid ground you have no need for a flotation device. In the seat back ahead of you, you will find a useful book of information that you are welcome to take with you after the flight. Our in flight movie tonight is the classic "The Plane Crash." If you require a snack during your flight, feel free to munch on the thing next to you."

Matthew grabbed the book in the seatback ahead of him just as the engines roared to life and the creaking plane took off into the pitch black night. Matthew was so tired he could not keep his eyes open and in the darkness, fell asleep.

The crackling sound of the intercom woke Matthew. *"As you exit the plane, make sure to gather all of your belongings. Anything left behind will be eaten by the flight attendants."*

Matthews looked around and noticed no one on board. He looked at his watch which read one minute after midnight. He looked out of the window and saw his hometown airport.

His family was delighted to have their Daddy home early to enjoy Halloween. Matthew knew that no one would believe his story so he kept it to himself. He gave his youngest daughter the book he took from the seatback on the plane, its title; FUN CAMPFIRE STORIES.

He reflected back on the last announcement he heard as he exited the plane, *"Thank you for flying Halloween Airlines. We hope you enjoyed giving us the business as much as we enjoyed taking you for a ride."*

A few parting thoughts

If your campfire story session needs a little relief, than there is nothing better than a closing joke or two. Following are a few of my favorite ones.

What kind of monster can fit on the end of your finger?

The bogey man

•

What do you call a good looking, polite, well mannered, kind and gentle monster?

A failure

•

Mommy, Mommy am I really a vampire?

Hurry up and drink your soup before it clots.

What does a vampire fear the most?

Tooth decay

•

What can you find between Godzilla's toes?

Slow runners

•

Monster 1 says, "That girl over there is rolling her eyes at me."

Monster 2 says, "Then you had better roll them back since she might need them later."

•

Why do cemeteries have fences around them?

Because people are dying to get in.

•

When is it bad luck to meet a black cat?

When you are a mouse.

Why don't mummies take vacations?

Because they are afraid that they will relax and unwind.

•

What goes Ha-ha-ha...THUD?

A skeleton laughing his head off.

•

What did Dracula say after hearing all these jokes?

They bite.

About the Author

John Bradshaw is a graduate of Furman University, former
United States Army Officer, former State of South Carolina
SITCON member, licensed private pilot, Black Belt in Karate
and business owner.
He is married to Alicia and they have three boys, Adam,
Christopher and Spencer
Visit John's website at www.eaglewingsbradshaw.com

Other published works:
FUN CAMPFIRE GHOST STORIES
FUN CAMPFIRE STORIES ANTHOLOGY

Made in the USA
Lexington, KY
09 July 2016